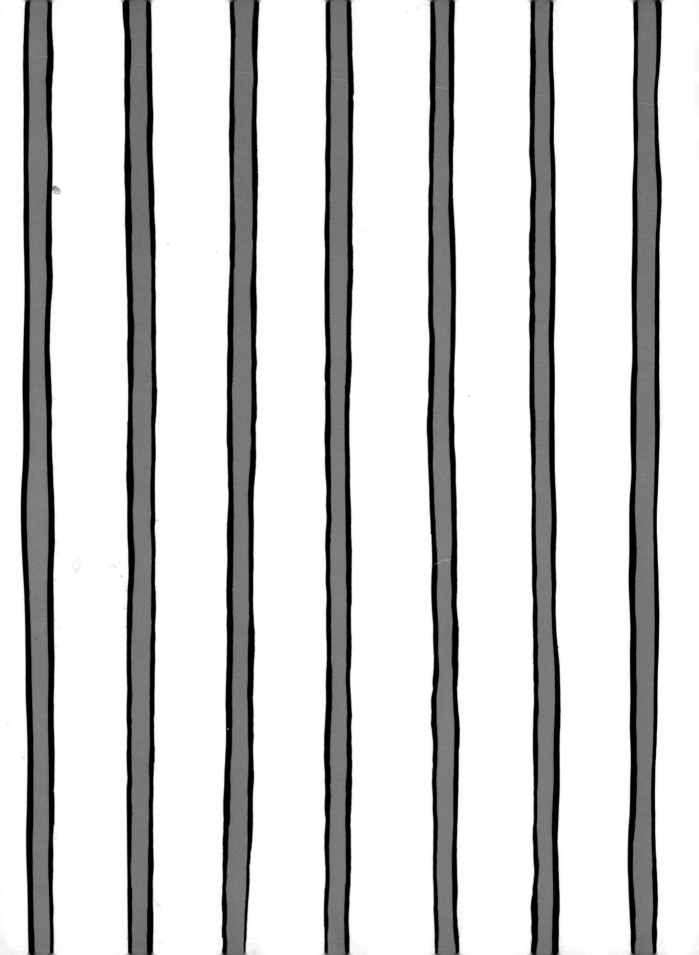

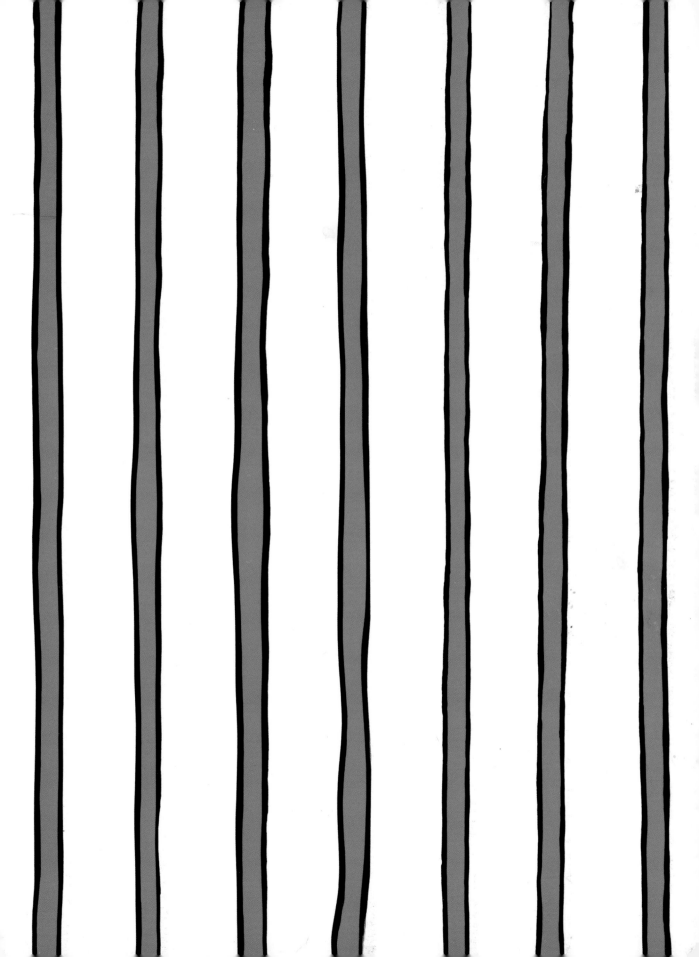

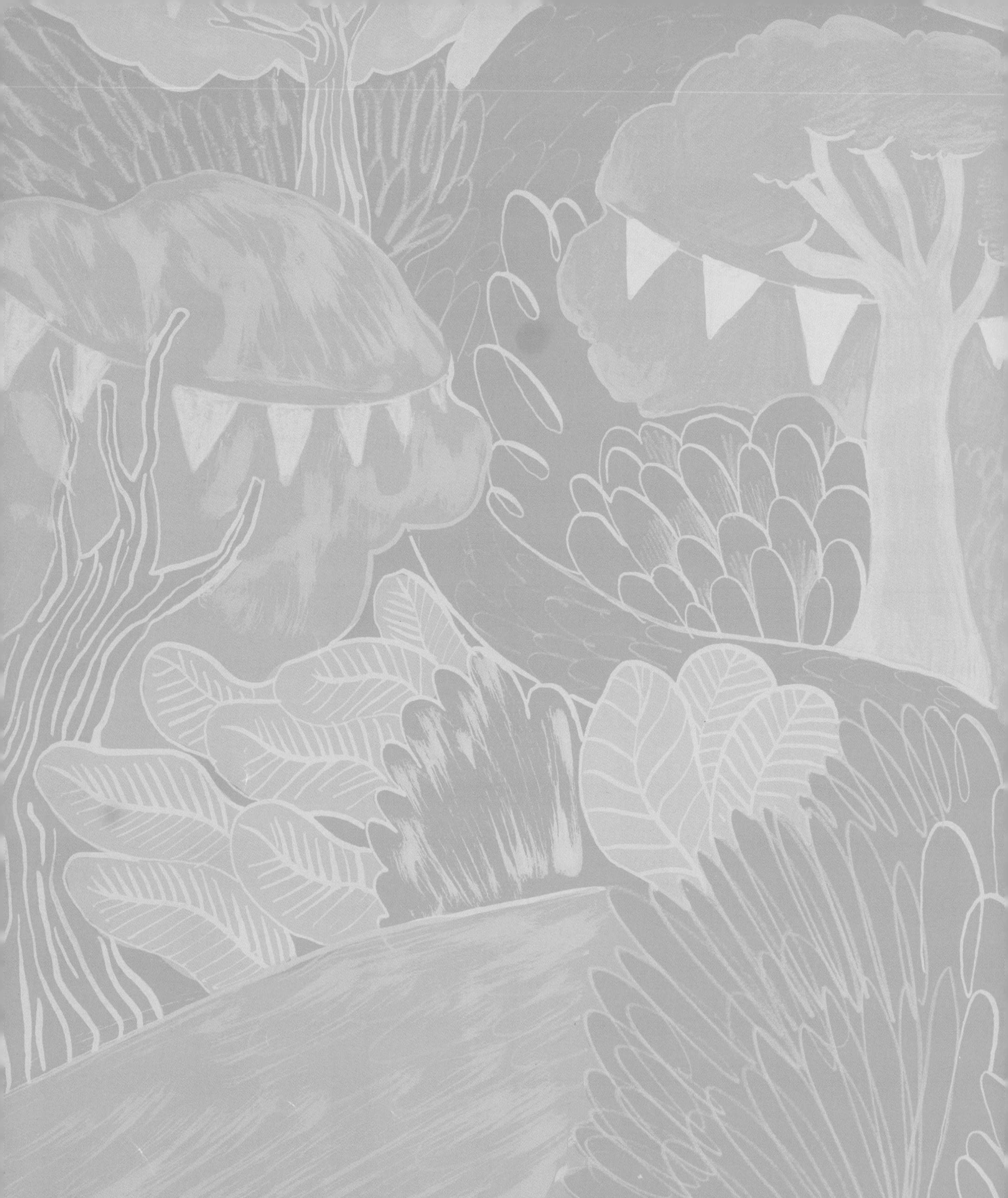

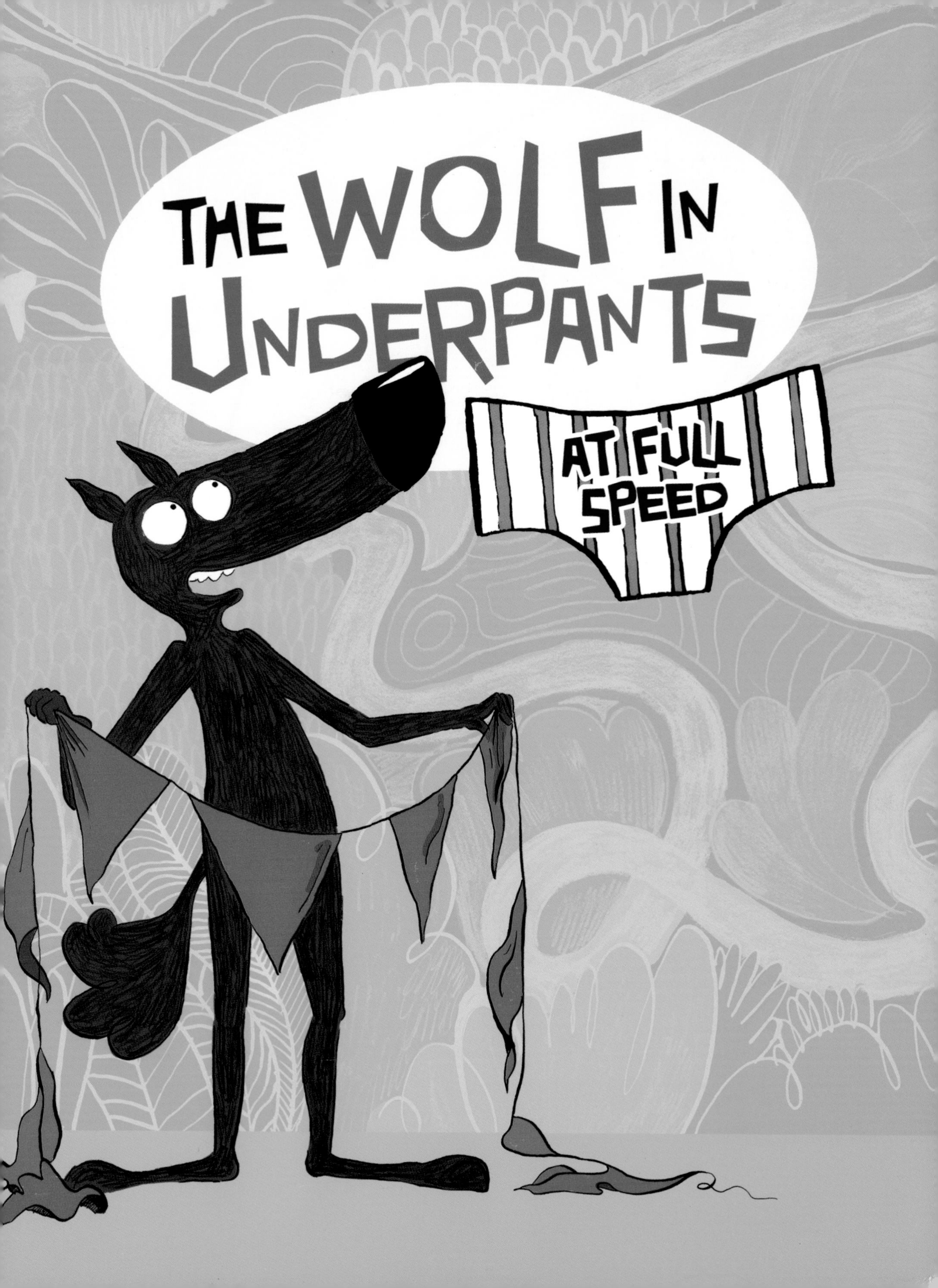
THE WOLF IN UNDERPANTS
AT FULL SPEED

Story by Wilfrid Lupano
Art by Mayana Itoïz
With the friendly artistic participation of Paul Cauuet
Translation by Nathan Sacks

First American edition published in 2021 by Graphic Universe™
Published by arrangement with Mediatoon Licensing - France
Le Loup en slip hip hip!
© Dargaud Benelux (Dargaud-Lombard S.A.) 2018—Lupano, Itoïz, and Cauuet. All rights
reserved. Original artistic director: Philippe Ravon.
www.dargaud.com

Graphic Universe™
An imprint of Lerner Publishing Group, Inc.
241 First Avenue North
Minneapolis, MN 55401 USA

For reading levels and more information, look up this title at www.lernerbooks.com.

Main body text set in Stick-A-Round. Typeface provided by Pintassilgoprints.

Library of Congress Cataloging-in-Publication Data

Names: Lupano, Wilfrid, 1971- author. | Itoïz, Mayana, 1978- artist. | Cauuet, Paul, 1980-
    artist. | Sacks, Nathan, translator.
Title: The wolf in underpants at full speed / story by Wilfrid Lupano ; art by Mayana Itoïz,
    with the friendly artistic participation of Paul Cauuet ; translation by Nathan Sacks.
Other titles: Loup en slip hip hip!. English
Description: First American edition. | Minneapolis : Graphic Universe, 2021. | Series: The wolf in
    underpants | Audience: Ages 7-11 | Audience: Grades 2-3 | Summary: "It's race day in the
    forest, but a surly chickadee has ruined the event's posters! When the Wolf learns why the
    little bird feels left out, he hatches a plan to launch it to victory" —Provided by publisher.
Identifiers: LCCN 2020021367 (print) | LCCN 2020021368 (ebook) | ISBN 9781728412979
    (library binding) | ISBN 9781728420233 (paperback) | ISBN 9781728417530 (ebook)
Subjects: LCSH: Graphic novels. | CYAC: Graphic novels. | Wolves—Fiction. | Forest animals—
    Fiction.
Classification: LCC PZ7.7.L86 Wp 2021 (print) | LCC PZ7.7.L86 (ebook) | DDC 741.5/973—dc23

LC record available at https://lccn.loc.gov/2020021367
LC ebook record available at https://lccn.loc.gov/2020021368

Manufactured in the United States of America
1-48541-49042-9/25/2020

THE WOLF IN UNDERPANTS

AT FULL SPEED

Wilfrid Lupano

Mayana Itoïz
and
Paul Cauuet

Graphic Universe™ • Minneapolis

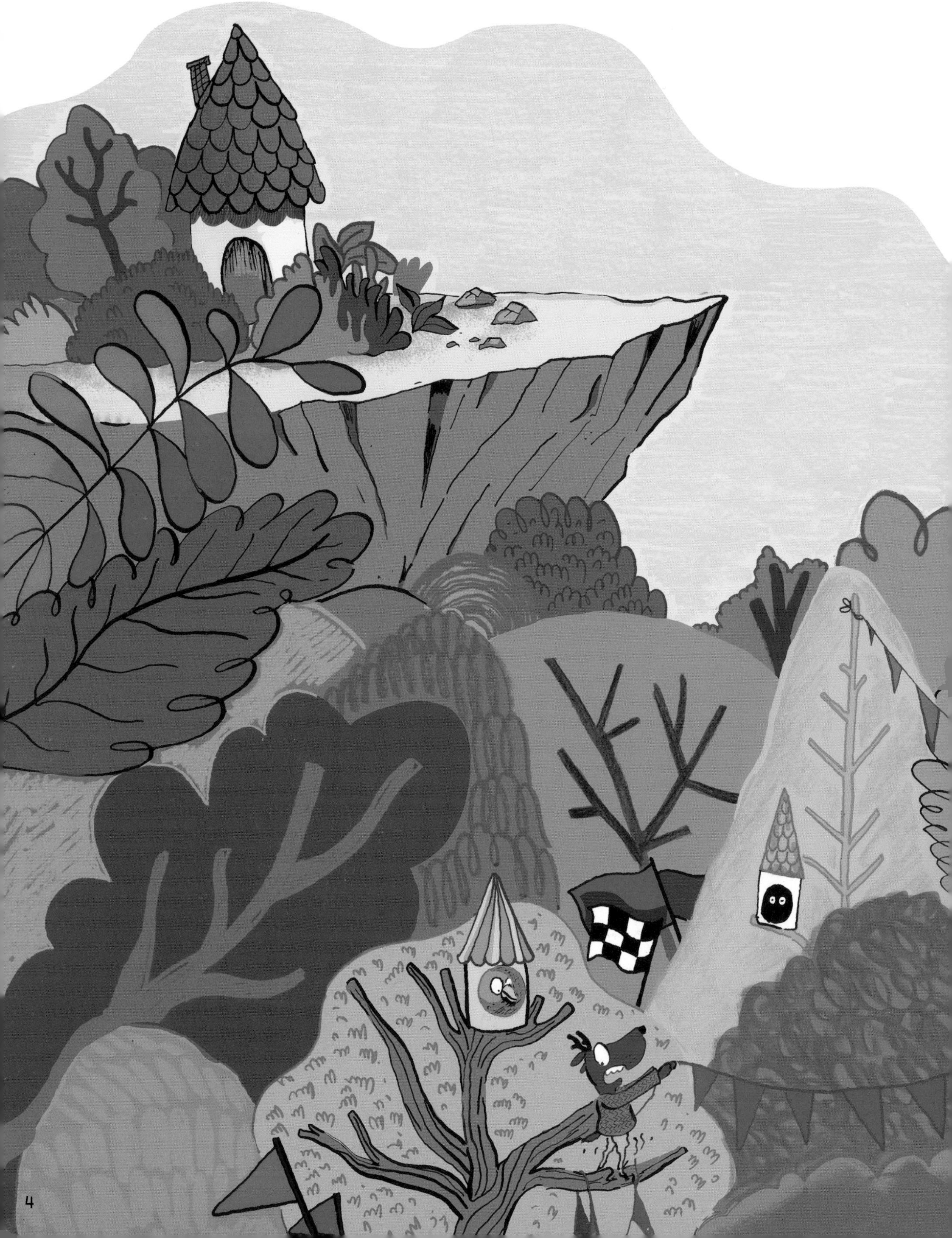

IT'S AN EXCITING DAY IN THE FOREST!
EVERYONE'S TAKING OUT PENNANTS AND
POM-POMS, BECAUSE TODAY IS . . .

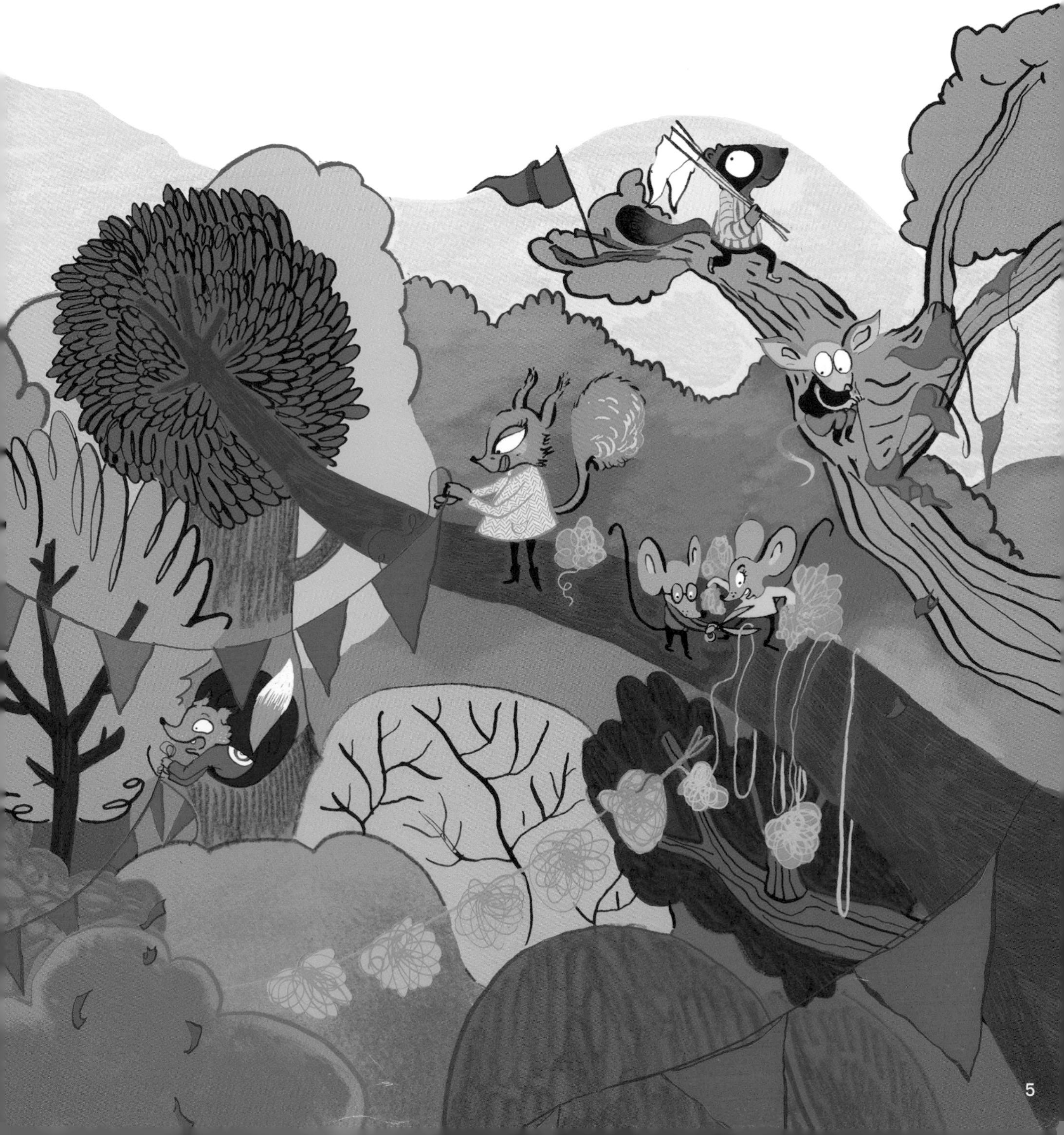

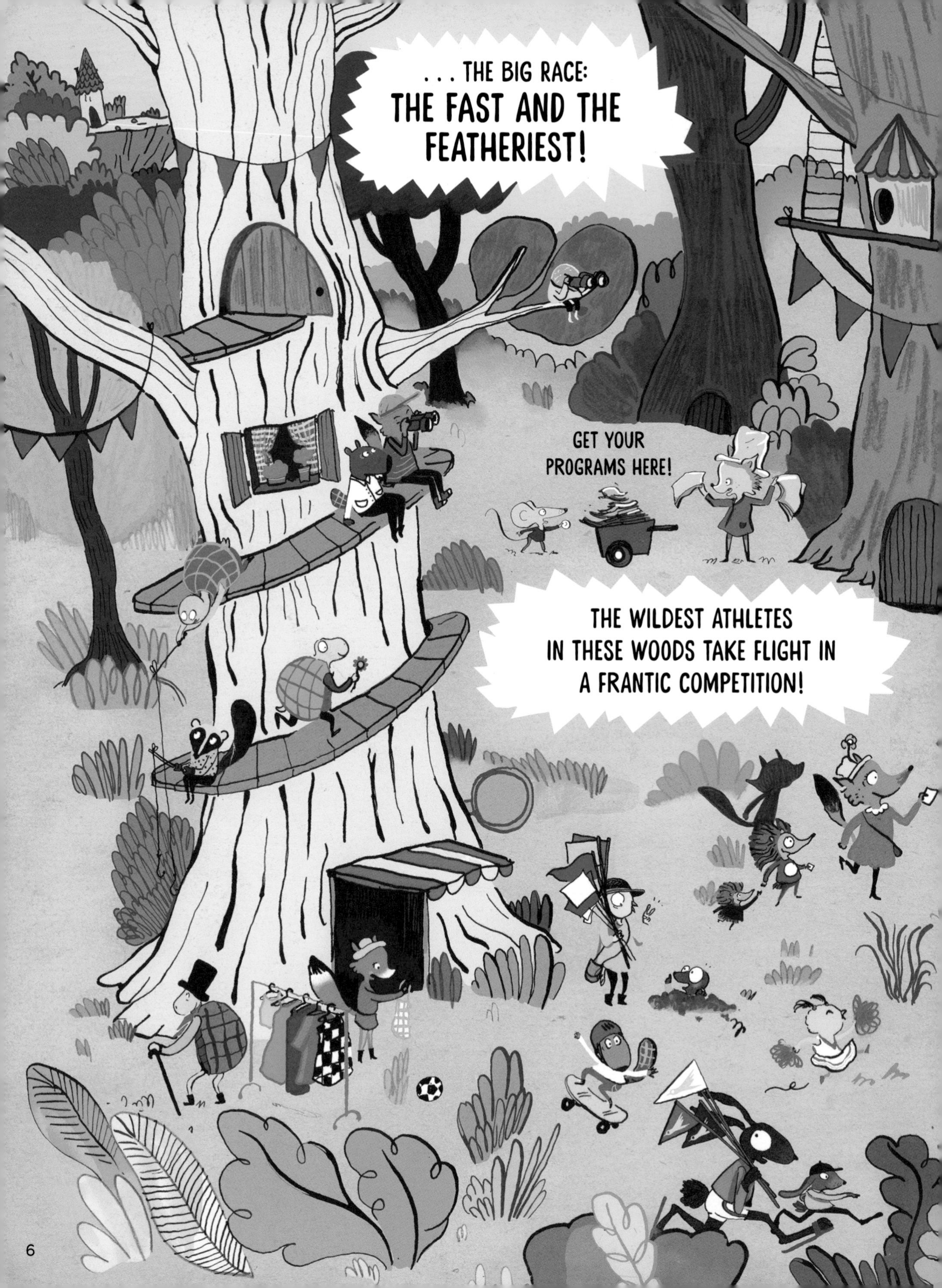
. . . THE BIG RACE:
THE FAST AND THE FEATHERIEST!
GET YOUR PROGRAMS HERE!
THE WILDEST ATHLETES IN THESE WOODS TAKE FLIGHT IN A FRANTIC COMPETITION!

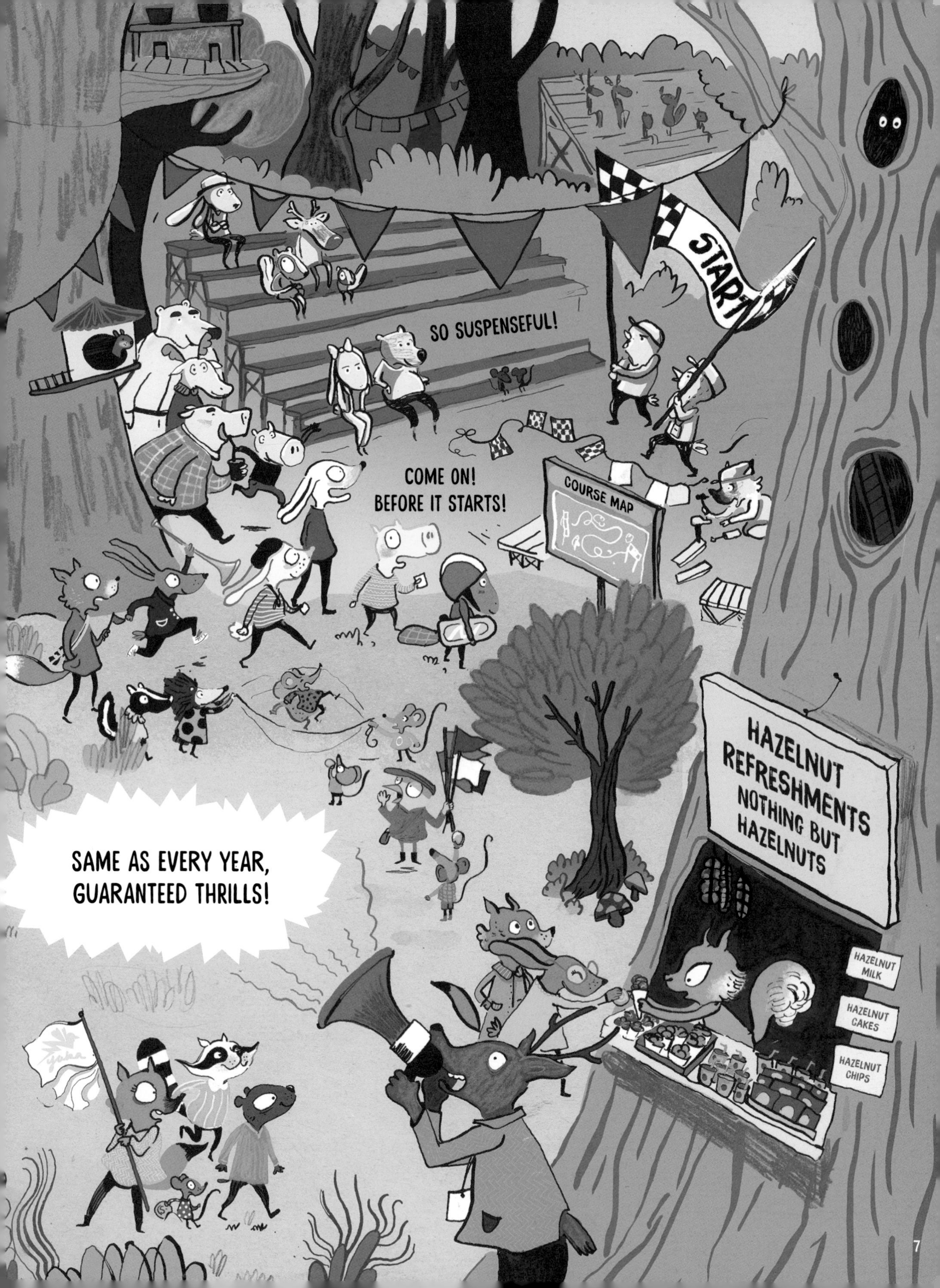
START
SO SUSPENSEFUL!
COME ON!
BEFORE IT STARTS!
COURSE MAP
SAME AS EVERY YEAR,
GUARANTEED THRILLS!
HAZELNUT
REFRESHMENTS
NOTHING BUT
HAZELNUTS
HAZELNUT MILK
HAZELNUT CAKES
HAZELNUT CHIPS

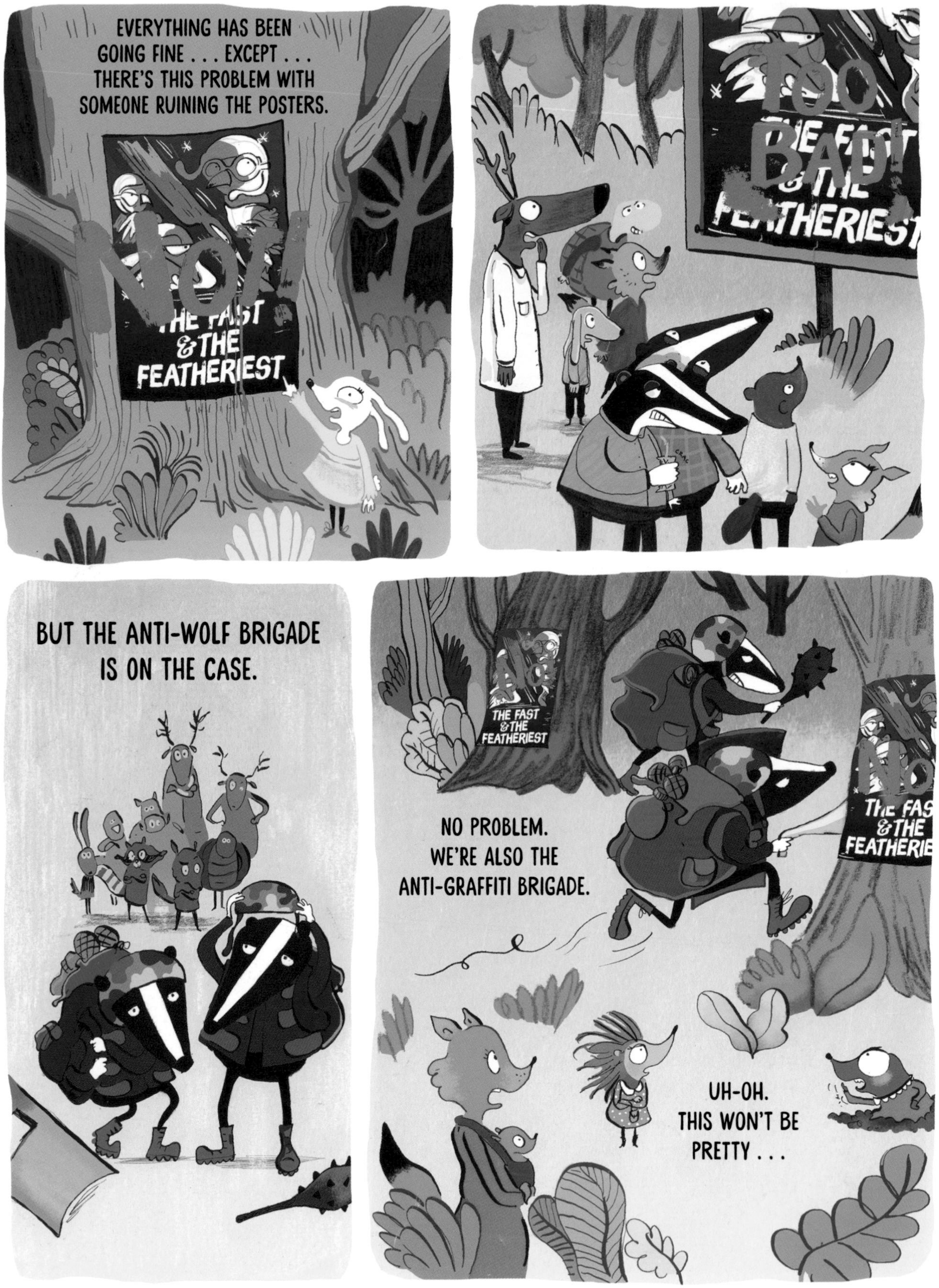
EVERYTHING HAS BEEN GOING FINE . . . EXCEPT . . . THERE'S THIS PROBLEM WITH SOMEONE RUINING THE POSTERS.
NO!
THE FAST & THE FEATHERIEST
TOO BAD!
THE FAST & THE FEATHERIEST
BUT THE ANTI-WOLF BRIGADE IS ON THE CASE.
THE FAST & THE FEATHERIEST
NO PROBLEM. WE'RE ALSO THE ANTI-GRAFFITI BRIGADE.
UH-OH. THIS WON'T BE PRETTY . . .

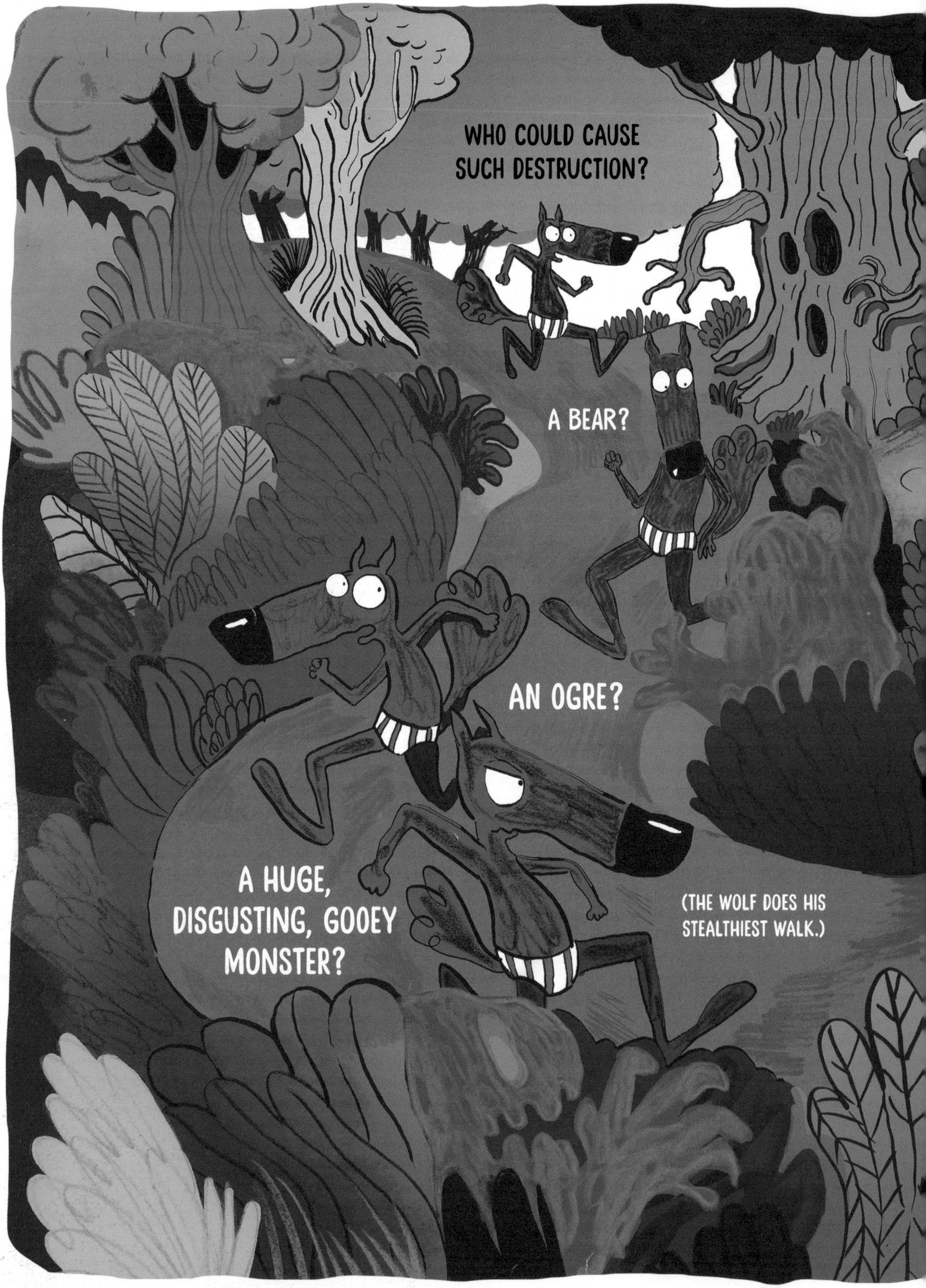
WHO COULD CAUSE SUCH DESTRUCTION?
A BEAR?
AN OGRE?
A HUGE, DISGUSTING, GOOEY MONSTER?
(THE WOLF DOES HIS STEALTHIEST WALK.)

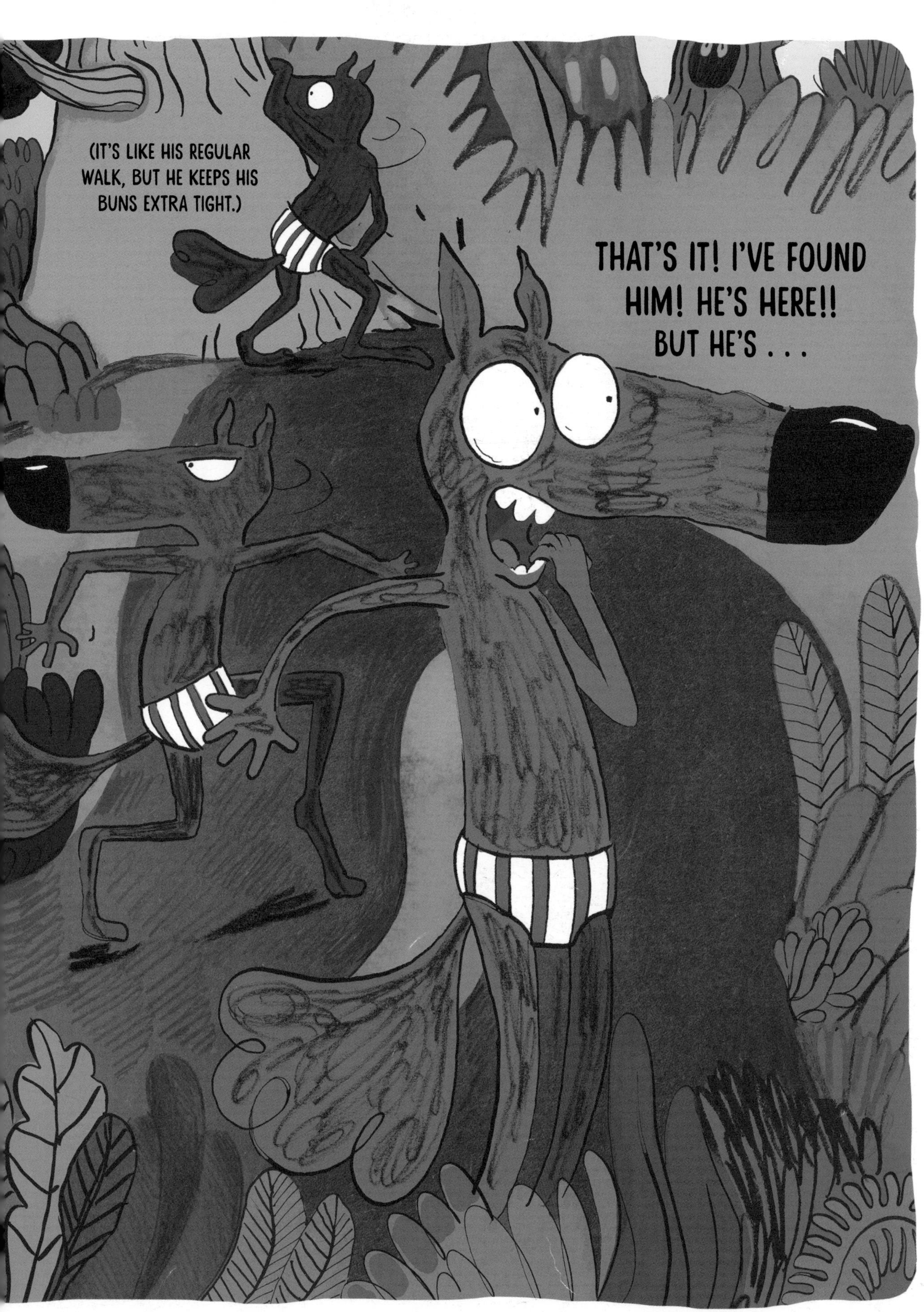
(IT'S LIKE HIS REGULAR WALK, BUT HE KEEPS HIS BUNS EXTRA TIGHT.)
THAT'S IT! I'VE FOUND HIM! HE'S HERE!! BUT HE'S . . .

WHEN I WAS LITTLE, I DREAMED ABOUT BEING THE BIG HERO OF THE FAST AND THE FEATHERIEST.

SO I TRAINED AND I TRAINED . . .

AND NOW HERE I AM. NOTHING WORKED. **LIFE STINKS!**

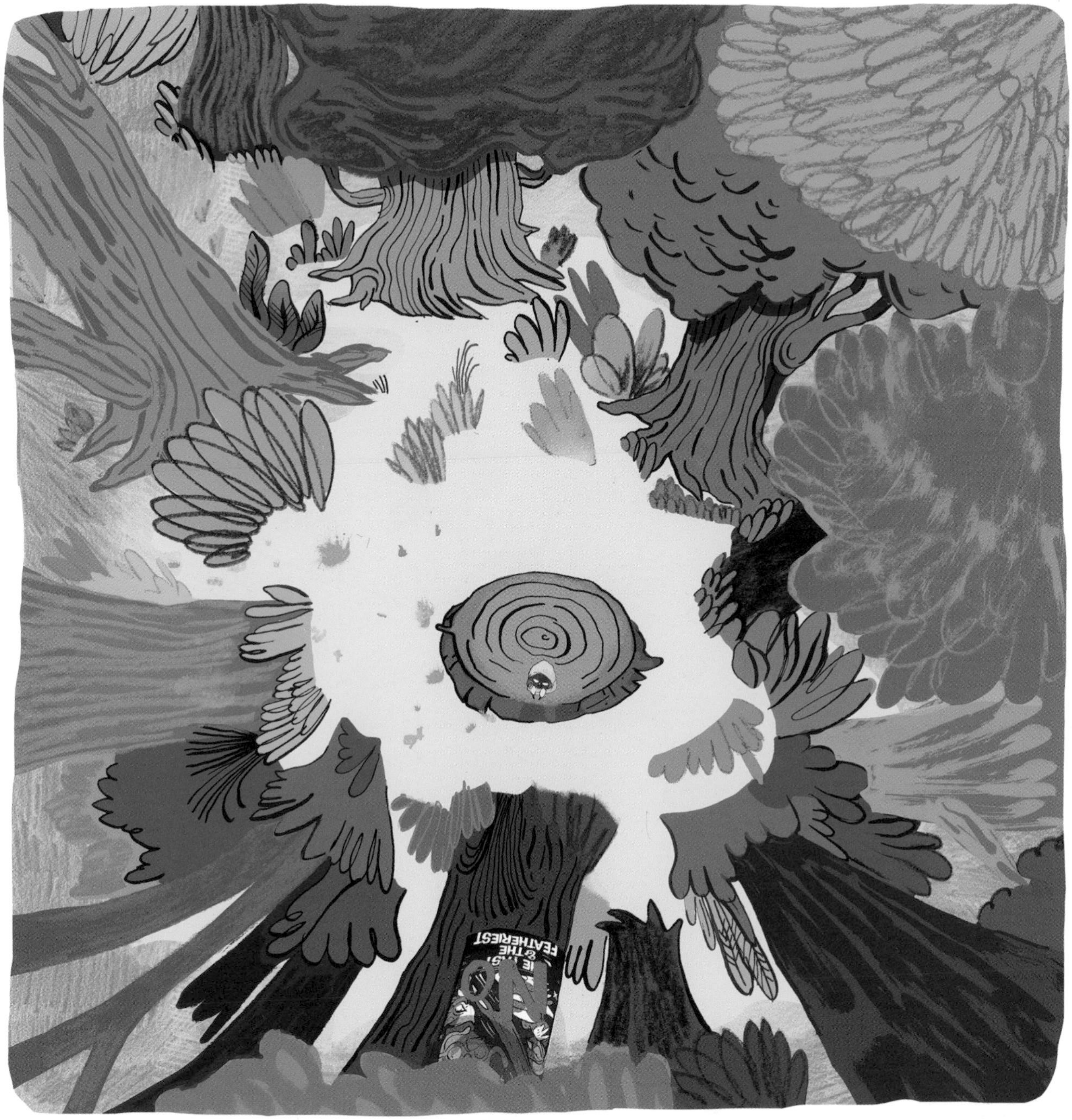

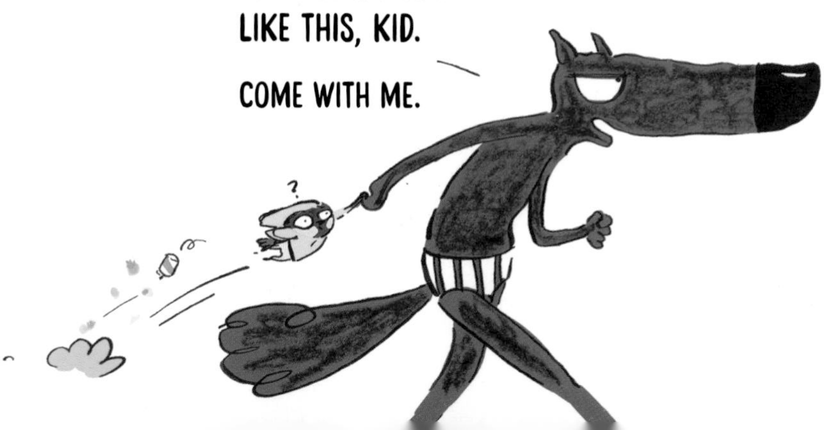
I CAN'T LEAVE YOU
LIKE THIS, KID.
COME WITH ME.

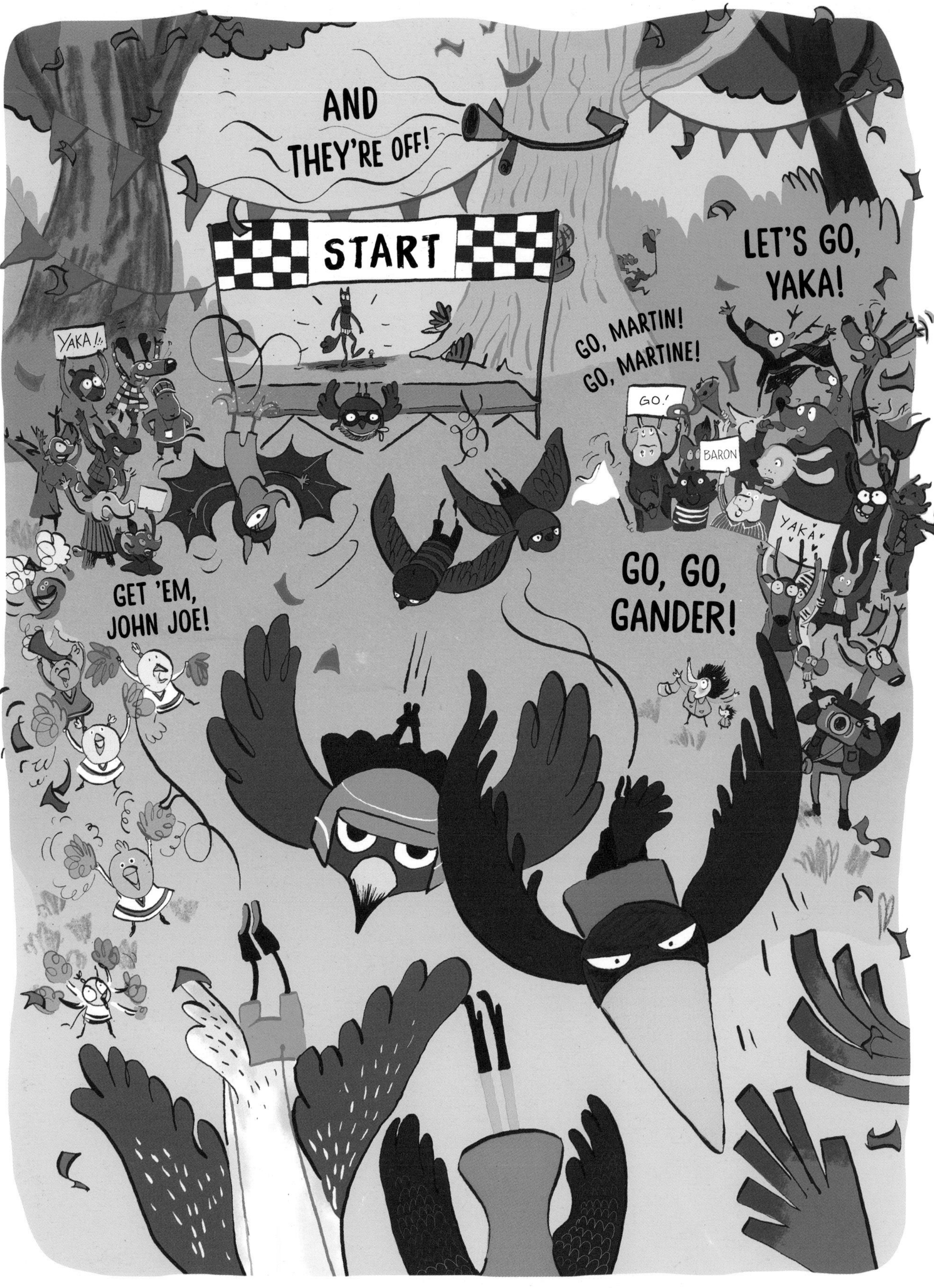
AND THEY'RE OFF!
START
YAKA!!
GO, MARTIN! GO, MARTINE!
LET'S GO, YAKA!
GO!
BARON
YAKA
GET 'EM, JOHN JOE!
GO, GO, GANDER!

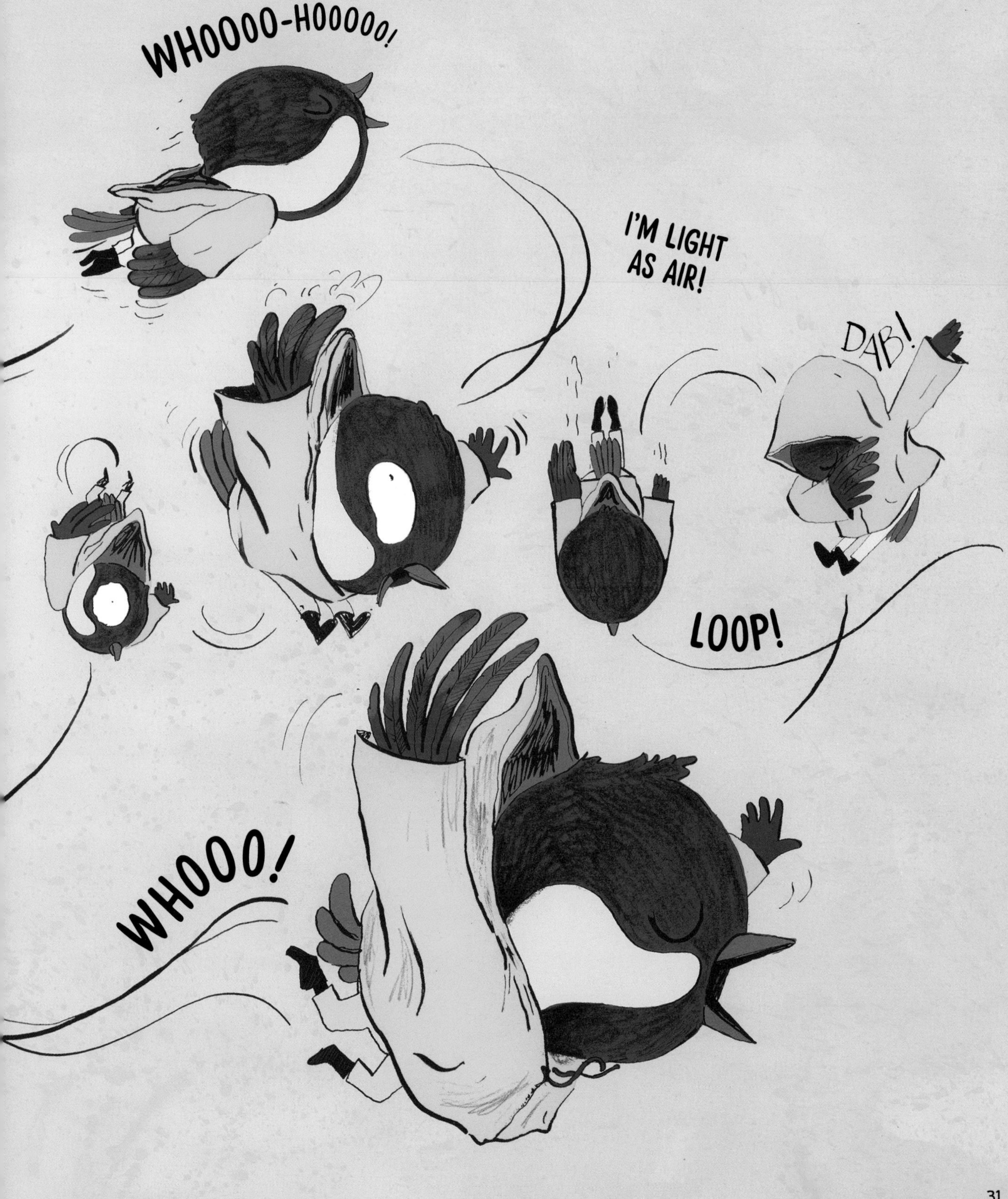
WHOOOO-HOOOOO!
I'M LIGHT AS AIR!
DAB!
LOOP!
WHOOO!

ABOUT THE CREATORS

WILFRID LUPANO

Wilfrid Lupano was born in Nantes, in the west of France, and spent most of his childhood in the southwestern city of Pau, France. He spent his childhood reading through his parents' comic book collection and enjoying role-playing games. He studied literature and philosophy, receiving a degree in English, before he began to script comics. He has written numerous graphic novels for French readers, including the series *Les Vieux Fourneaux* (in English, *The Old Geezers*). With this series, Lupano and Paul Cauuet first developed the idea that would become *The Wolf in Underpants*. Lupano once again lives in Pau after spending several years in the city of Toulouse.

MAYANA ITOÏZ

Mayana Itoïz was born in the city of Bayonne, in the southwest of France, and studied at the institut supérieur des arts de Toulouse (School of Fine Arts in Toulouse), where she worked in many different mediums. In addition to being an illustrator and a cartoonist, she has taught art to high school students. She lives in the Pyrenees, near France's mountainous southern border, and splits her time between art, family, and travel.

PAUL CAUUET

Paul Cauuet was born in Toulouse and grew up in a family that encouraged his passion for drawing. He was also a fond reader of classic Franco-Belgian comics such as *Tintin* and *Asterix*. He studied at the University of Toulouse and went on to a career as a cartoonist. Cauuet and Wilfrid Lupano first collaborated on an outer-space comedy series before working together on *Les Vieux Fourneaux* (*The Old Geezers*).

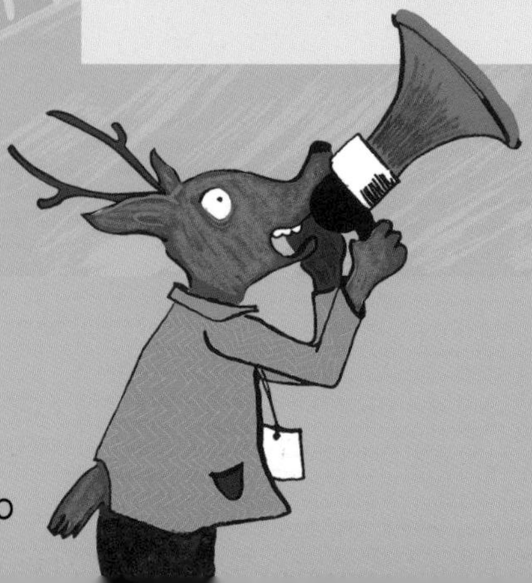

ABOUT THE TRANSLATOR

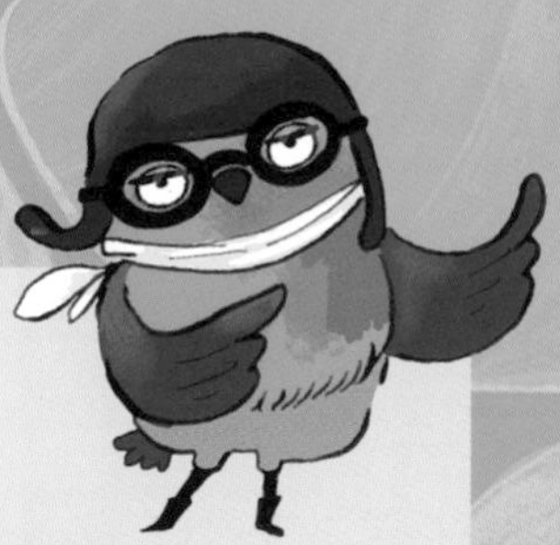

NATHAN SACKS

Nathan Sacks is a writer, editor, and translator from Ames, Iowa, who lives in Los Angeles. He has written fiction and nonfiction children's books and translated several graphic novels from French to English.

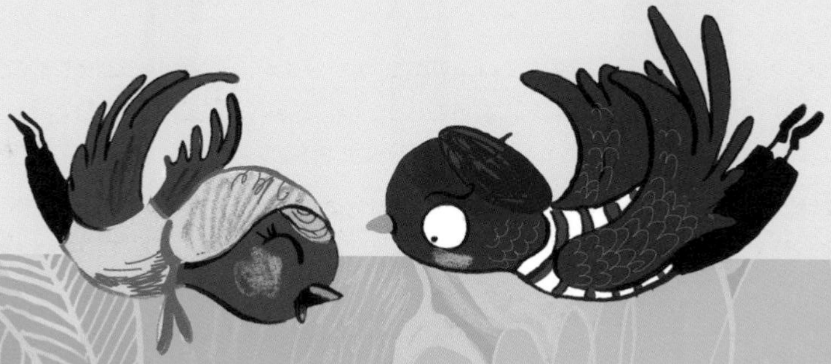

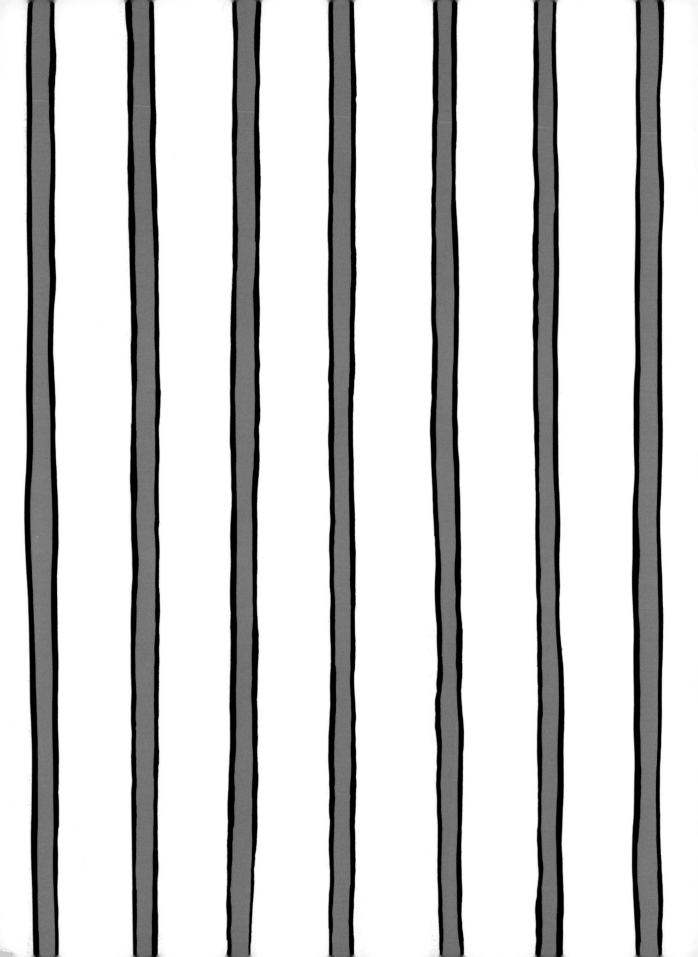

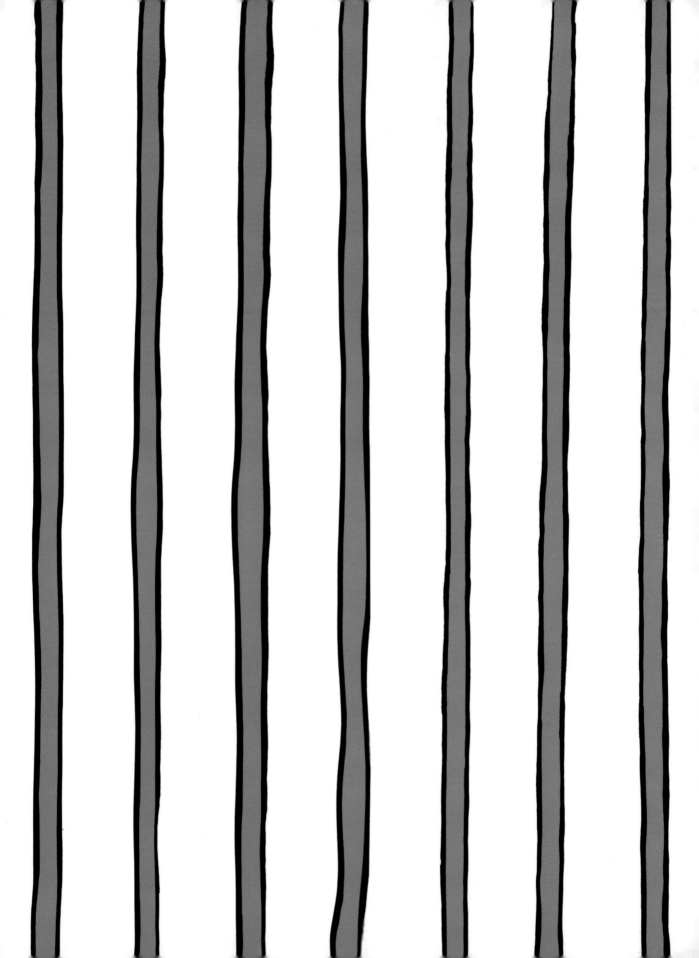